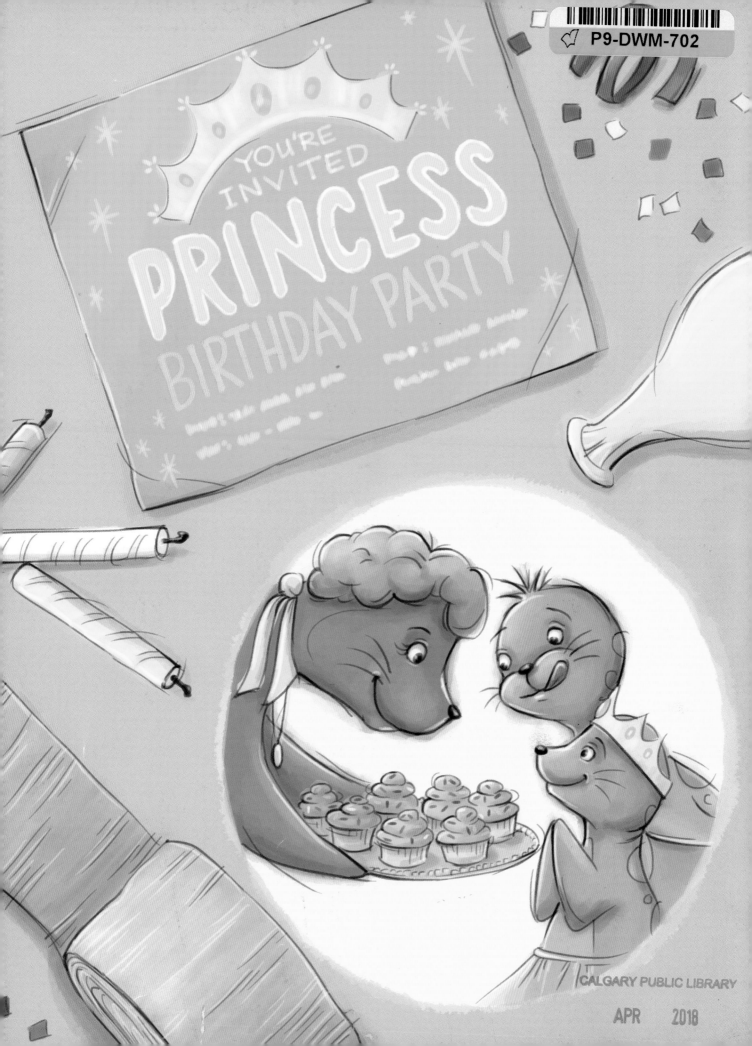

Alfred A. Knopf · New York

KLONDIKE, DO NOT EAT THOSE CUPCAKES!

Amanda Driscoll

Hello, Klondike.

Yes, those cupcakes look delicious.

Yes, I know you love cupcakes.

A lot.

But you heard your mother: NO cupcakes until your sister's birthday party.

Yes, Klondike, it is hard to wait.

Really.

Truly.

Very.

Extremely.

Hard.

To.

Wait.

But you can do it.

No, Klondike, you cannot have just one bite.

Not even a nibble.

I saw that.

Pretend the cupcakes are squid sandwiches . . .

Or tubeworm tacos . . .

Or curried crabs.

Oh, right. Seals love
squid sandwiches,
tubeworm tacos,
and curried crabs.

My highly trained guard dog, Bruiser, will protect these cupcakes.

That's very disappointing, Bruiser.

Look, Klondike!
A magician is here
for the party!

Check that there
is nothing in his hat
and nothing up
his sleeves.

Now watch closely
as he pulls an Arctic
hare out of his hat.

Hocus pocus!

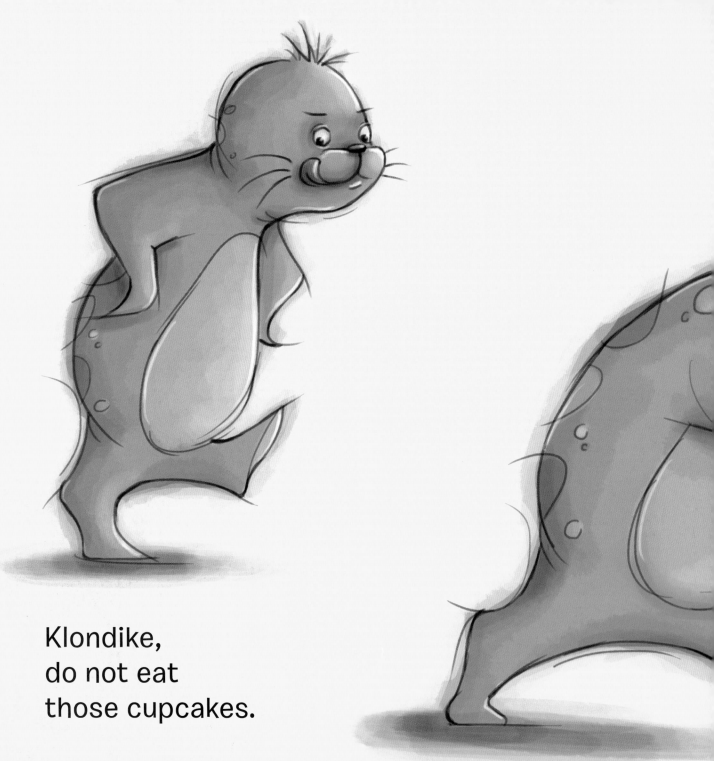

Klondike,
do not eat
those cupcakes.

Oh, boy.

Klondike, DO NOT
eat those cupcakes!

YIKES.

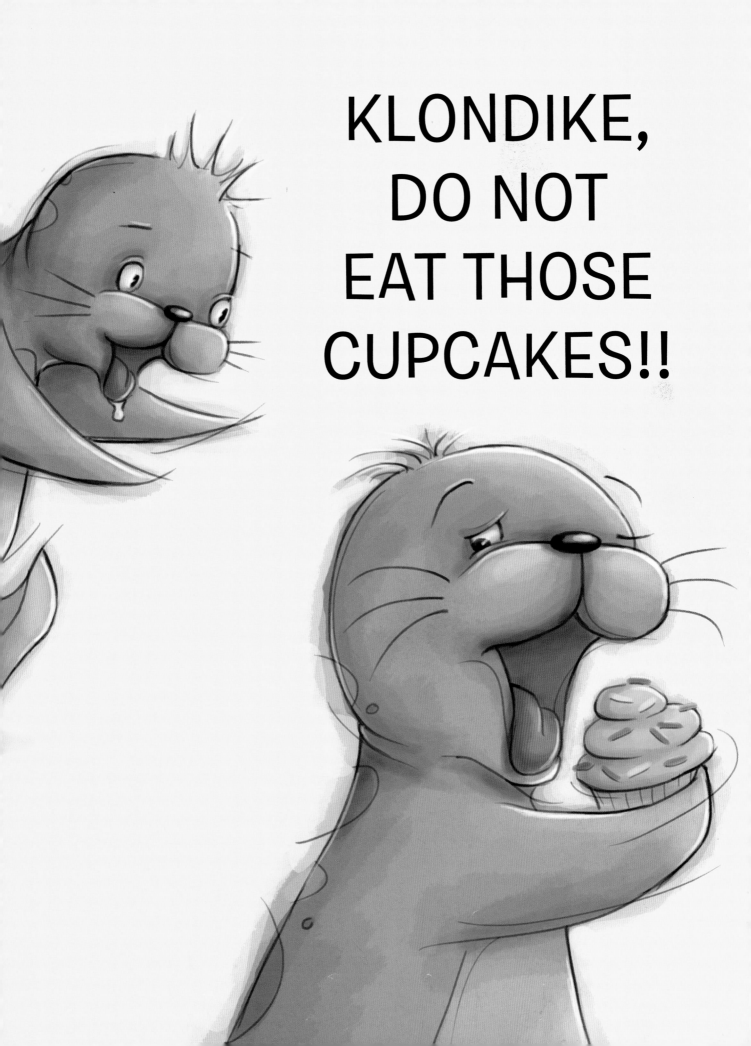

Klondike. You ate those cupcakes.

Don't even try
to deny it.

The dog did not make you do it.

Uh-oh. Here comes your mother.

And look at your poor sister. There will be no cupcakes at her party . . . no candles to blow out . . . no wishes to make.

Unless . . .

Now, *this* I
have to see.

Nicely done, Klondike.

Yes, I know you love your sister. A lot.

Oh, you made a treat for me, too?

That's very . . . um . . . uh . . . thoughtful.

Hey, Klondike. It's finally party time!
You know what that means.

KLONDIKE, EAT THOSE CUPCAKES!

In memory of Will

THIS IS A BORZOI BOOK PUBLISHED BY ALFRED A. KNOPF
Copyright © 2018 by Amanda Driscoll

All rights reserved. Published in the United States by Alfred A. Knopf,
an imprint of Random House Children's Books, a division of Penguin Random House LLC, New York.
Knopf, Borzoi Books, and the colophon are registered trademarks of Penguin Random House LLC.

Visit us on the Web! rhcbooks.com
Educators and librarians, for a variety of teaching tools, visit us at RHTeachersLibrarians.com

Library of Congress Cataloging-in-Publication Data
Names: Driscoll, Amanda, author, illustrator.
Title: Klondike, do not eat those cupcakes! / Amanda Driscoll.
Description: First edition. | New York : Alfred A. Knopf, [2018] | Summary: "Klondike isn't supposed to eat
the cupcakes until his sister's birthday party . . . but can he wait that long?" —Provided by publisher
Identifiers: LCCN 2016019643 (print) | LCCN 2016059576 (ebook) | ISBN 978-1-524-71316-4 (trade) |
ISBN 978-1-524-71317-1 (lib. bdg.) | ISBN 978-1-524-71318-8 (ebook)
Subjects: | CYAC: Behavior—Fiction. | Cupcakes—Fiction. | Birthdays—Fiction. | Seals (Animals)—Fiction.
Classification: LCC PZ7.D7866 Klo 2018 (print) | LCC PZ7.D7866 (ebook) | DDC
[E]—dc23

The illustrations in this book were created using pencil sketches painted in Adobe Photoshop.

MANUFACTURED IN CHINA
January 2018   10 9 8 7 6 5 4 3 2 1   First Edition
Random House Children's Books supports the First Amendment and celebrates the right to read.

Chocolate Chip Cupcakes
by Klondike

Makes about 20 cupcakes

INGREDIENTS:

1⅔ cups all-purpose flour
1 cup sugar
¼ tsp. baking soda
1 tsp. baking powder
¾ cup salted butter, room temperature

3 tsp. vanilla extract
3 egg whites
½ cup sour cream
½ cup milk
2 cups semi-sweet chocolate chips

INSTRUCTIONS:

1. Preheat oven to 350°.
2. Whisk together flour, sugar, baking soda, and baking powder in a large mixing bowl.
3. Add butter, vanilla, egg whites, sour cream, and milk, and mix on medium speed just until smooth. Don't overmix. Stir in chocolate chips.
4. Fill cupcake liners until they are about 3/4 full.
5. Bake 18-22 minutes.
6. Allow to cool before adding frosting. Frost and decorate as desired.

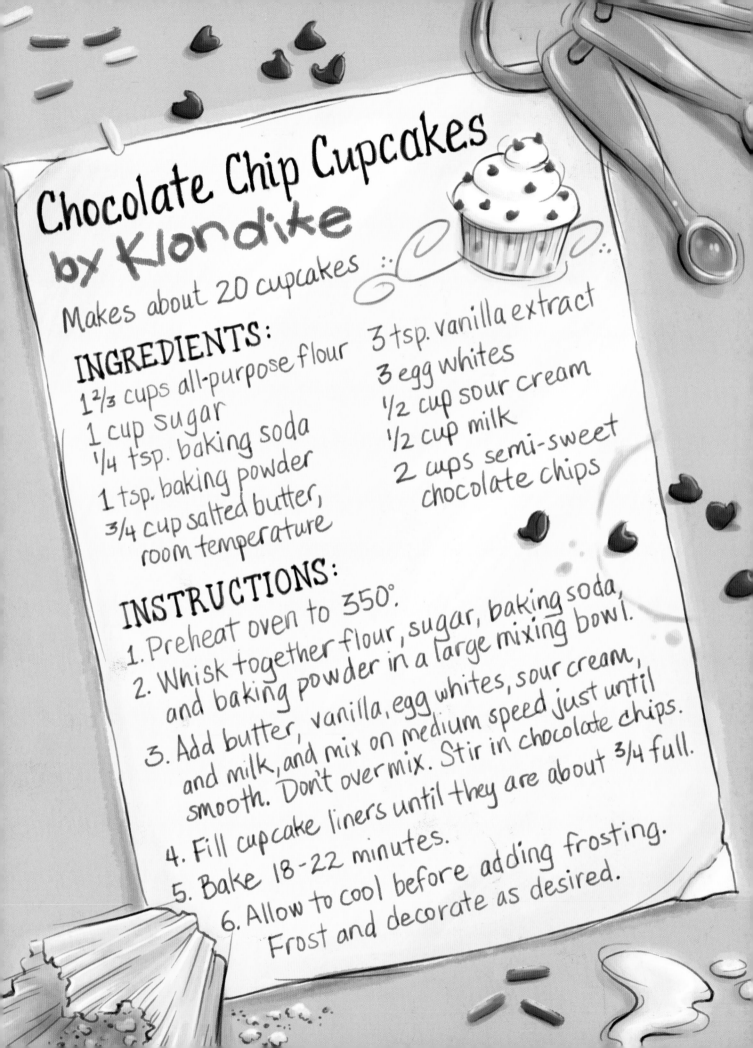